Peter
5 years old

Elias
5 months old

Conrad
3 years old

Marissa
86 years old

Halle
3 years old

Erika
42 years old

Flora
3 years old

THIS BALL WAS DRAWN BY

~~~~~~~~~~~~~~~~~~~~~~~~~~~

First American Edition published in 2009 by Enchanted Lion Books, 201 Richards Street, Studio 4, Brooklyn, NY 11231 Originally published in Finnish as Pom Pom © Anne Peltola 2005 All rights reserved in accordance with the provisions of the Copyright Act 0f 1956 as amended A CIP record is on file with the Library of Congress ISBN-10: 1-59270-085-3 ISBN-13: 978-1-59270-085-1 Printed in China by South China Printing Co. Ltd.

ANNE PELTOLA

BOING BOING

ENCHANTED LION BOOKS

I made a picture of a ball.
Red and round.
I called it Boing Boing.
It was so beautiful that I wanted
to show it to everyone!

We
laughed so hard
that Boing Boing bounced up into the sky.
As we laughed, it soared higher and higher,
up to where escaped balloons and airplanes fly.
Boing Boing went up and up
until a gray cloud stopped it.
Then lickety-split,
it drip-drip-dropped all the way down...

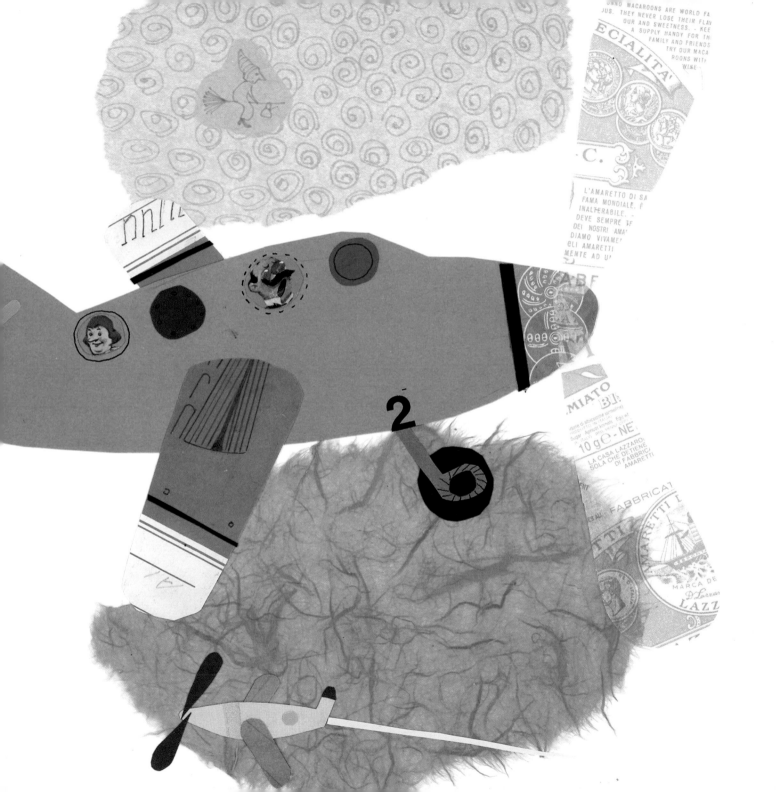

Boing Boing
landed near a wolf on vacation. He was fixing
his shiny red car by the side of the road. It was in
ship-shape except for a tire that looked like spilled
black paint. "Oh, wow!" howled Wolf in surprise.
"A spare tire that's almost good as new!"

vroom vroom

hummed the car. Boing Boing
was off to the beach. Wolf drove
up and down, left and right,
around and around, both the
right way and the wrong way,
until Boing Boing rolled off—
ready for a new adventure.

Boing Boing bounced along, bouncing at last
onto the back of a dog before

bOIngING...

...into a sand box, where a cat found it.
Cat loved Boing Boing's bright color
and brought it home for lunch.

Now Cat had a new plate – a round red plate, which made eating from it just a little bit tricky. Cat ate raw fish, beans, rice, berries and a gazillion other things from her new plate. Then she fell asleep swishing her tail and sweeping Boing Boing off the table…

Oh, no!

Boing Boing bounced
away, making a
somersault as it flew.
Bibbity, bobbity, boing!

A fox in the fields thought he was dreaming about a flying cherry. He let out a big "O" to see if he would wake up.

Then two sheep chased Boing Boing around
and around until their heads were spinning.

"It's a balloon," bleated one sheep. "Let's catch it!"

"It will be our new toy," baaaed the other sheep.

They threw Boing Boing into the air and rolled it on the ground, trying to catch it.

Then everything turned UPSIDE DOWN and Boing Boing bounced away, out of sight.

"Mommy," cried Boing Boing.
"I'm lost. It's dark in here and
I'm all alone. I want to go home!"

Just then a bear came into the place where Boing Boing was lost. "Oh my, look at that! A yummy red sweet!" exclaimed Bear. "But wait, what's this, candies don't cry!"

"That's right, I'm not a candy," said Boing Boing.

"You see, I'm a round red ball and I don't know how to find my way home."

"That's why I'm crying."

"I'll help you," said Bear. He felt a little like crying too.

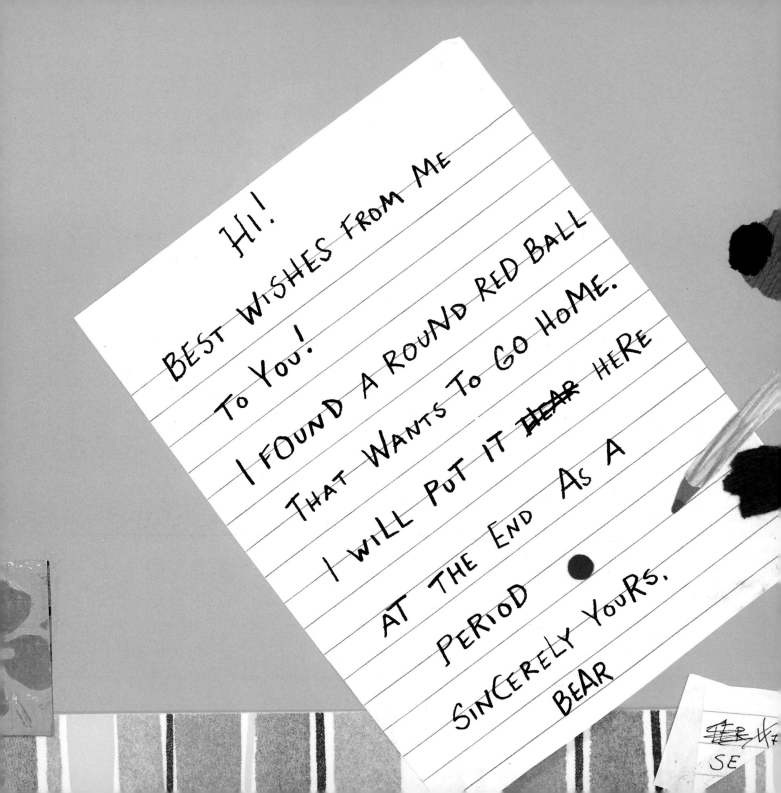

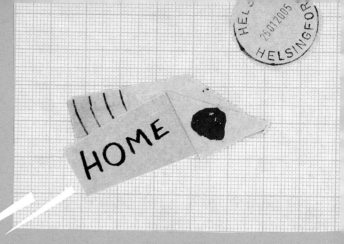

Bear wrote his letter and wrote HOME on the
envelope.
Then he squashed a blueberry on as a stamp
and sent it off.

Air Mail

Boing Boing flew with the wind.
Over oceans and fields, past trees
and birds, right to where its own
bed and teddy bear were waiting.

I was **overjoyed** when Boing Boing returned home! I was happy that my ball had gone on a trip to see the world, but I was happiest of all that it had come back to me. Soon we will go on new adventures together, and there will be many more stories to tell. But it's late now and I'm falling asleep.
Good night!

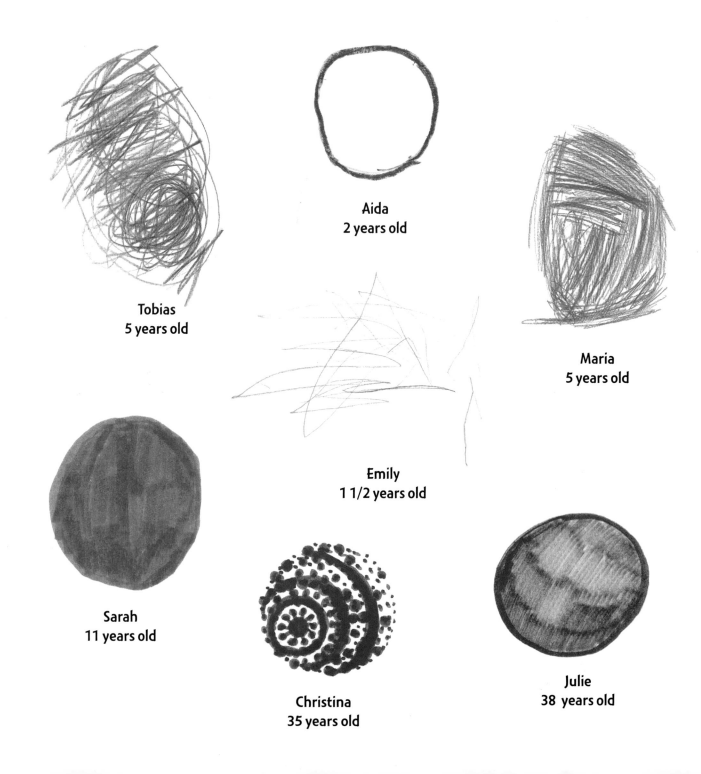

Tobias
5 years old

Aida
2 years old

Maria
5 years old

Emily
1 1/2 years old

Sarah
11 years old

Christina
35 years old

Julie
38 years old